ELEPHANTS DON'T SIT ON CARS

Grown-ups, in Jeremy James's experience, live
in a different world. They forget that the bathroom lock needs mending, have to be reminded
that the best tin of fruit is the one in the
middle of the bottom row, and refuse to believe
that elephants sit on cars. Uncles can sometimes
be more reasonable — Uncle Arthur, for instance,
who pays Jeremy James a visit in the middle
of the night — and the very occasional babysitter
who actually asks what Jeremy James would
like to do instead of telling him what he ought
to like to do. . . Jeremy James is a natural
troublemaker whose misdeeds more often than
not rebound on himself and are therefore all
the funnier to read about.

ELEPHANTS DON'T SIT ON CARS

By

David Henry Wilson

Illustrated by Patricia Drew

CHATTO & WINDUS · LONDON

Published by
Chatto & Windus Ltd
40-42 William IV Street
London WC2N 4DF

*

Clarke, Irwin & Co Ltd
Toronto

*For
Chris,
Jenny,
and (of course) J.J.*

British Library Cataloguing in Publication Data
Wilson, David Henry
  Elephants don't sit on cars.
  I. Title
  823'.9'lj   PZ7.W/

  ISBN 0-7011-2273-0

Printed and bound in Great Britain by
Redwood Burn Ltd
Trowbridge & Esher

Contents

The Elephant on Daddy's Car

'Mummy,' said Jeremy James, 'there's an elephant sitting on Daddy's car.'

'Yes, dear,' said Mummy, eyes fixed on hands fixed on dough fixed on table.

'Mummy, why is the elephant sitting on Daddy's car?'

'I expect it's tired, dear. It'll probably get up and go away soon.'

'Well, it hasn't,' said Jeremy James two minutes later. 'It hasn't got up. The car's gone down, but the elephant hasn't got up. Mummy, do you think I ought to tell Daddy?'

'No, no, leave your father,' said Mummy, 'you know he hates being interrupted when he's working.'

'Daddy's watching a football match on television.'

'If Daddy says he's working, he's working.'

'Well, there's an elephant sitting on his car,' said Jeremy James.

Mummy thumbed sultanas into the dough to make eyes and noses.

'And the car doesn't look very happy about it,' said Jeremy James.

'Jeremy James,' said Mummy. 'Elephants don't sit on cars.'

'Well this one does.'

'Elephants don't sit on cars. If Mummy says elephants

don't sit on cars, dear, then elephants don't sit on cars.'

'But. . .'

'They don't. Finish! Now play with your train set.'

Jeremy James sat on the carpet, and played with his train set, and thought about the elephant on Daddy's car, and thought about how stubborn Mummies can be when they want to be, and how if he was a Mummy and his son said there was an elephant on Daddy's car, he would say 'What a clever boy,' and 'Thank you for telling me,' and 'Here's some money for an ice-cream.' Instead of just 'Elephants don't sit on cars.'

'Goal!' said the television set in the sitting-room.

'Goal!' said Daddy, hard at work.

And the elephant was still sitting on Daddy's car.

'Mummy,' said Jeremy James, for the latest development really couldn't be ignored. 'Mummy, the elephant has just done its Number Two all over Daddy's car.'

But Mummy's face merely twitched like a fly-flicking elephant's ear, and she said nothing.

'Gosh, and *what* a Number Two! Mummy, you should see the elephant's Number Two! Mummy, why do elephants do such big Number Twos? I can't do a Number Two like that! Mine isn't even a thousandth as big as that! *What* a Number Two!'

'Jeremy James, if you go on talking like that, I shall send you straight to bed. Now play with your train set, and let's have no more elephant talk, and certainly no more about Number Twos. Do you hear?'

'Yes, Mummy.'

No Number Twos. Anyone would think that Number Twos were unhealthy. Only look what happened when you didn't do a Number Two. Then it was: 'Jeremy James, have you done your Number Two? You haven't done your Number Two? Then sit there until you have.'

8

Now tell them an elephant's done his Number Two on Daddy's car, and suddenly it's rude. Why can't grown-ups make up their minds?

Jeremy James played with his train set.

Jeremy James looked out of the window. The elephant was gone.

'Mummy,' said Jeremy James.

'What is it now?' said Mummy, half in and half out of the oven.

'The elephant's gone.'

'Hmmph.'

That was a typical grown-up word: 'Hmmph.' It was for grown-ups only, and meant whatever they wanted it to mean. Jeremy James had tried to use a 'Hmmph' once himself. Mummy had said, 'Have you done your Number Two?' (at one of those times when Number Two wasn't rude) and he'd replied 'Hmmph', because that was how grown-ups got out of awkward questions like Will you buy me something nice today, or Why can't I have a toy racing car like Timothy's? Only Jeremy James obviously didn't know how to use it, because Mummy told him to speak properly, even though he'd said 'Hmmph' perfectly properly.

Daddy came out of the sitting-room, with his face as long as an elephant's nose.

'They lost,' said Daddy. 'Right at the end. An own goal.'

Then Daddy leaned on the kitchen doorpost as he always did when he'd been working (and sometimes when he *was* working), and watched Mummy working, presumably to make sure she was doing everything right. Jeremy James had tried leaning on the doorpost once and saying, as Daddy always ended up by saying, 'Will it be long, dear?' But instead of getting Mummy's normal

'Hmmph', he'd had a 'Now don't you start!' and been sent off to play with his train set, which he was sick of anyway.

'Will it be long, dear?' said Daddy.

'Hmmph,' said Mummy.

'Now don't you start,' said Jeremy James quietly.

'An own goal,' said Daddy. 'Right at the end.'

'Was that goal Number Two?' asked Jeremy James.

'I don't know what's got into that child,' said Mummy.

Daddy elbowed himself upright off the doorpost, took one hand out of one pocket ('Take your hands out of your pockets, Jeremy James!'), yawned, and announced, 'Maybe I'll go and clean the car.'

Mummy didn't say, 'There won't be time before tea,' though Daddy waited quite a long time for her to say it, and so Daddy eventually left the kitchen, crossed the dining-room, entered the hall, opened the front door, and went out of the house.

Jeremy James stood at the window and wondered what new words Daddy would use.

Daddy didn't use any words. Daddy's mouth fell open, and then Daddy came back to the house, opened the front door, entered the hall, crossed the dining-room, and held himself up by the kitchen doorpost.

'The car!' said Daddy. Then his mouth opened and shut several times as if he'd just been pulled out of the water. 'The car!' he said again.

'What's the matter with it?' asked Mummy, spreading hand-cream over the bread.

'It's ruined! It. . . it. . . it's ruined! It looks as if it's been completely squashed! Completely and utterly squashed!'

'Oh John,' said Mummy, who only called Daddy John when she was very upset or when she wanted some

11

money, 'Oh John, there. . . there isn't. . . um. . . sort of
. . . dung all over it as well, is there?'

'Yes,' said Daddy, 'there jolly well is! I've never seen
anything like it, either. Must have been a herd of cows
dancing on the thing!'

'It wasn't a herd of cows,' said Jeremy James, 'it was
an elephant. And I saw it. And I told Mummy, but she
wouldn't listen.'

'An elephant!' said Daddy. 'You saw an elephant on
the car?'

'Yes,' said Jeremy James, 'and I saw it do its Number
Two as well.'

'Then why the. . . .. didn't one of
you tell me?'

'Hmmph!' said Mummy, and Jeremy James played
with his train set.

Jeremy James Goes Shopping

'I'm going shopping,' said Mummy. 'Do you want to come with me?'

'Will you buy me something nice?' said Jeremy James.

'You can't expect me to buy you something nice every time I go shopping,' said Mummy. 'I don't go shopping just to buy you something nice, and in any case it's the end of the month, so I can't afford it.'

'Are you going to buy cornflakes?' asked Jeremy James.

'Yes,' said Mummy.

'Well I'd sooner go without my cornflakes, and have something nice instead,' said Jeremy James.

'Hmmph,' said Mummy. 'Get your coat on.'

'I'm quite warm, though, Mummy.'

'Get your coat on.'

That, thought Jeremy James, is typical. Just because *she's* cold, *I* have to put a coat on.

Jeremy James and Mummy went to the shops. They walked. Jeremy James would much rather have gone by bus, but Mummy said they would come back by bus when they had the shopping to carry. It was healthier to walk. It was also cheaper to walk. So Jeremy James pretended he was a bus, and steered in and out of people till he almost steered straight into an old lady, and then Mummy told him to walk properly,

so he became a guardsman instead.

The trouble with Mummy when she went shopping was that she liked all the wrong shops. Boring clothes shops and china shops and food shops especially. She only bought things in the food shops, but she spent hours in the clothes shops touching things, and hours outside the china shops gazing in as if it were the zoo. Even in the food shops she spent hours touching and gazing. She fingered every packet of cheese, opened every box of eggs, weighed every piece of meat. The only thing she didn't spend hours on was tins of fruit, and tins of fruit were the one thing Jeremy James did like looking at. Apart from boxes of sweets and bars of chocolate and packets of cake. And Mummy didn't spend any time on them either. Mummy didn't really seem to have much idea about shopping.

Next to the food supermarket was a toy shop. It was a new toy shop, and its windows were full of games and soldiers and tanks and guns and footballers and bows and arrows, and a few silly things for girls. Jeremy James noted all this as they walked past the toy shop, and he pointed it out to Mummy. He said, 'Oh look, Mummy, look at all the games and soldiers and tanks and guns and footballers and bows and arrows, and those silly things for girls.' Mummy said, 'Hmmph,' and wouldn't stop because they would be late for dinner, or something. Jeremy James followed her with his feet, leaving his eyes behind, and bumped into a fat woman with a fur coat and a poodle. The fat woman with the fur coat and the poodle said something a bit like 'Hmmph!' but with rather more 'ph' than 'hmm', and Jeremy James said 'Ouch' and ran after Mummy, while the fat woman looked angry and moved her lips as if she was talking.

Mummy started picking up chickens. They were frozen chickens in paper wrappings, and they all looked alike, but Mummy studied them very carefully, one after another. Jeremy James fixed his eye on one particular chicken Mummy had just put down, and there was no doubt whatsoever that she picked the same one up again a minute later.

'You've seen that one already,' said Jeremy James. 'I know, 'cos I've been watching it.'

Mummy didn't seem to hear.

'Mummy, won't we be late for dinner, or something?' said Jeremy James.

But examining chickens seemed really to make Mummy rather hard of hearing. Jeremy James wandered off to the tinned fruit department. He looked up at the coloured walls of mouth-watering pictures: pineapples, pears, peaches, cherries, raspberries, strawberries, and mandarin oranges — sweet mandarin oranges — all in their own juice which was deliciously cold after you'd put the tin in the fridge for a while. The only trouble with tinned fruit was that you always wanted a second helping, and Mummy always said 'No' because there was nothing left. They should make the tins a bit bigger so you could have a second helping. When he was grown up, of course, Jeremy James would buy *two* tins, just to make sure, but he'd suggested that to Mummy and she'd said something about tinned fruit not growing on trees, and that apparently meant no.

In front of the wall of juicy pictures were big wire thingamebobs all full of tins just like the tins up against the wall. People took tins from the thingamebobs and put them in their trolleys, leaving the others standing intact. This seemed odd to Jeremy James, because although the tins were all the same, the tins up against the wall *looked* nicer. They were sort of regular and more juicy-looking. Grown-ups probably don't notice these things, because when they're taking tins of fruit they're in a hurry and simply go for the nearest one, which is always in the wire thingamebob. The same with cakes and bars of chocolate — they just take whatever's nearest because they're not interested in interesting things. They only pick and choose when it's boring things like meat or cheese or chickens.

The more Jeremy James studied the wall of tins, the

16

more obvious it became that those were the *best* tins. That was why the people who owned the shop put them further away — they were probably saving them for themselves when the shop closed. After all, when Mummy bought fresh pears, peaches, oranges, apples and so on, some were always nicer than others, and she always insisted they should eat the nasty ones first. That must be the way grown-ups did things. Nasties first. It was the same with dinner and dessert. She never let him have dessert till he'd finished dinner. And he had to have his bath before he could have his bed-time story. And he had to tidy his room before he got his piece of chocolate. Nasties first, that was the rule. And so the best tins of fruit were those against the wall, and the best tin of all must be the one most difficult to get at — the last tin that anybody could reach. It must be that tin there (he was in front of the mandarin orange department) — the tin in the middle of the bottom row.

Jeremy James imagined saying to Mummy, 'Mummy, this is the best tin of mandarin oranges in the whole shop.' And Mummy would say he was a clever boy, and she might buy him an ice-cream even though it was the end of the month. In fact she might make it his regular job — choosing the best tin of fruit every time they went shopping. Jeremy James smiled to himself. Life is simple when you use your brain. Jeremy James looked round quickly to make sure the shop people weren't looking, because you could be quite certain they would try to stop him taking the best tin of mandarin oranges in the whole shop. No one was looking. Jeremy James eased past the wire thingamebob. Jeremy James bent down. Jeremy James put his hand round the best tin of mandarin oranges in the whole shop. Jeremy James pulled. The best tin of mandarin oranges didn't move. Of course it didn't move — there were two more tins resting on it holding it down. And so with his left hand Jeremy James pushed the two holding-down tins, and with his right hand he pulled out the best tin of mandarin oranges.

And then a strange and terrible thing happened. The wall of tins seemed to do a kind of knees-bend. And then the tins started falling down. First of all they fell from all round the best tin which wasn't there any more, and then they fell all over the place. Some of them fell on Jeremy James, but he quickly jumped out of the way, and stood behind the wire thingamebob, watching. Tins were bouncing and rolling everywhere, and it wasn't just mandarin oranges — peaches, pears and pineapples joined in as well. And the people in the shop all stopped moving around and turned to look in the direction of the tins of fruit, and two or three shop people came hurrying along with pale faces and frowning eyebrows, and an old lady pointed at her foot and limped away muttering, and a baby cried, and more tins fell and rolled, and a very big shop man in a grey suit started giving orders and making the other shop people run around, and there were veins standing out in his forehead, and his eyes were bulgy, and he didn't look a very nice man, and his bulgy eyes settled on Jeremy James, and Jeremy James decided he'd better go back to Mummy. He was rather glad, when he turned round, that Mummy was already there.

'Come on, Jeremy James,' said Mummy. 'We'll be late for dinner.' Or something. Mummy took the best tin of mandarin oranges in the whole shop out of Jeremy James's hand, and slipped it into her trolley, and pulled Jeremy James along — rather roughly, he thought — to the cash desk.

As they left the shop, Jeremy James looked back. The shop people were still picking up tins, and the man in the

grey suit still didn't look very nice. But Jeremy James knew why the man in the grey suit was angry. He'd wanted that tin of mandarin oranges for himself, that was why.

The Football Match

Every so often Daddy stopped working. That is to say, every so often Daddy admitted he had stopped working. Of course, he wasn't working when he was in bed, in the bath, in the kitchen, in the armchair, leaning on the doorpost, or watching television, but otherwise generally he *was* working. His study door was firmly closed, and from the study would come that profound stillness and silence of the man at work. You could sometimes hear a typewriter, too, but Daddy always said it was the bits in between the typewriter that were the real work, and the quieter he was, the harder he was working. That was what Daddy said.

But every so often, Daddy stopped working. And on Saturday afternoons he almost never worked. And on this particular Saturday afternoon, as on every other Saturday afternoon, he announced after lunch that he was going to take the afternoon off. There was, he had been led to believe, a football match on this afternoon, and as he felt in need of some fresh air, he might pop along to see it.

'Why don't you take Jeremy James?' said Mummy.

Daddy thought hard for a minute or two, wondering why he couldn't take Jeremy James, but it soon became clear from his silence that he couldn't find any particular reason. And so Jeremy James was wrapped up in his thickest sweater and his heaviest coat and his ear-warmingest ear-warmers, and went off hand-in-hand with Daddy, blowing clouds of dragon-breath over the winter landscape.

They didn't take the car because, said Daddy, it would be quicker to walk. Lots of cars went past them, soon leaving them far behind, but when Jeremy James pointed out that the cars were quicker than they were, Daddy simply murmured 'You'll see', so Jeremy James and he went on walking. When they got near the football stadium, the pavement began to get more and more crowded, and very soon they were walking in the road, and Daddy was quite right, because they then started passing cars which hooted angrily. Jeremy James wanted to let go of Daddy's hand so that he could be a racing car zooming in and out of the leg-jungle, but Daddy made him hold on tight; otherwise, as Daddy said, 'They'll turn you into a half-time message.'

Outside the ground itself, there were queues which were certainly the biggest queues in the world. The queues in Mummy's food shops weren't even queues compared with these queues. These were monster queues, with hundreds of thousands of people — most of them men, which made them even more different from the food-shop queues. A lot of the men looked very happy, and had bright scarves (mainly blue and white) round their necks, with big flowers (also blue and white) stuck in their coats. One or two men had rattles (also blue and white) which were a lot bigger than Jeremy James's old baby rattles that he had grown out of long ago. These rattles were so big you could never grow out of them, and they made a much louder noise than a thousand of Jeremy James's old baby rattles.

The queues moved a lot quicker than the food-shop

queues, and each time someone went into the football ground, there was a clickety-click, which turned out to be an iron bar you had to push through. When Jeremy James pushed through, it went clickety-click, just as it had done for the man in front of him, but really when you thought about it, there didn't seem much point, because you could have got into the ground much easier without the iron bar.

'I think we'll go in the stand,' said Daddy, 'it'll be more comfortable.' And so they joined another queue, which was much smaller than the first queue, and soon they were climbing up some steep steps, at the top of which was a man with a moustache and a red face who took Daddy's ticket. And then for the first time Jeremy James saw the football pitch. It was quite different to football pitches on the television, because this one was green, and very big. You certainly couldn't get this big green one on to the little television screen at home, and that was a fact.

'Come on, Jeremy James!' said Daddy, and pulled him along to a place where people had their feet. When Daddy and Jeremy James arrived, the people took their feet away, and Daddy sat down. Jeremy James sat down as well, though he thought it a bit funny to sit down where people normally put their feet. It was hard, too.

'We're better off in the stand,' said Daddy. 'You can see better, too.'

'Is this the stand, Daddy?' asked Jeremy James.

'Yes,' said Daddy.

'Well why are we sitting down, then?' asked Jeremy James.

'This is where you sit down,' said Daddy.

'Then why's it called the stand?' asked Jeremy James.

'Now, don't you start asking stupid questions,' said

Daddy. 'I haven't come here to give a lesson on semantics.'

Mummy, of course, would have said 'Hmmph', but Daddy often used long words that didn't exist when he couldn't answer a question. Semantics was one of his favourite words, though Jeremy James knew it was only the name of a tabby cat three doors away.

Someone was saying something over the loudspeaker. It sounded like 'Worple shob worple forby gambridge Number Two,' and Jeremy James assumed he was checking that the footballers had all done the necessary before the game started. Grown-ups had a thing about going to the lavatory before you did anything.

Then all of a sudden everybody shouted, and some men came running on to the field, kicking a ball. They were dressed in red and white, and most of the shouting wasn't very friendly. But when more men came running on to the field, kicking another ball, and all dressed in blue and white, even Daddy started shouting a funny sort of 'worp worp!' shout, as if he knew them.

'Are they your friends, Daddy?' asked Jeremy James.

'They're the home team,' said Daddy.

Jeremy James was quite sure he had never seen any of the men at home, but Daddy was shouting again, and it was best not to interrupt.

A man in black — 'Has his grandma died, Daddy?' said Jeremy James — blew a whistle, not nearly as well as Jeremy James could blow *his* whistle, everybody shouted again, and the men started kicking the ball and running round the field. Jeremy James watched for a little while, and Daddy told him the names of some of the men in blue, though Jeremy James didn't know any of them, and couldn't remember any of them once Daddy had told him. Daddy said the men were trying to

24

kick the ball into the net at the end of the pitch, but Jeremy James never saw anybody trying to kick the ball into the net at all. Most of the time the ball wasn't anywhere near the net, and the men seemed to be trying to kick it in any other direction *but* the net. Sometimes the men didn't even kick the ball, but kicked each other, and then everybody shouted and the man in black blew his whistle and waved his arms. Once the ball came up into the sitting-down stand, very near to Daddy, and Jeremy James reckoned even he could kick the ball closer to the net than that, but when he said so to Daddy, Daddy said the man wasn't trying to kick the ball into the net — and that made the whole thing even more confusing.

Nobody got the ball into the net, and the man in black at last blew his whistle, and the players walked slowly off the pitch. Daddy then started talking to the man next to him, and Jeremy James heard him say, 'The ref needs his blooming eyes tested.' So Jeremy James turned to the man next to him — who had glasses and a funny chin — and said, 'The ref needs his blooming eyes tested.' The man with glasses and a funny chin seemed a little surprised, so Jeremy James added, 'That's what my Daddy says.'

After some loud music and a lot of talking, the players came out again, and the man in black blew his whistle, and the running and kicking went on as before. Jeremy James noticed that when a man in blue kicked the ball or a man in red, the crowd was happy, and when a man in red kicked the ball or a man in blue, they lost their tempers and shouted nasty things. But obviously Daddy had made a mistake about the ball going into the net, because nobody seemed even to try and kick it in. Until hours and hours had gone by, and the man in black was looking at his watch as if he was learning to tell the time. And then suddenly one of the men in red kicked the ball very hard, and it went straight into the net.

'Oh good!' shouted Jeremy James. 'He got it in! He got it in the net, Daddy!'

And then all the people with blue and white scarves and blue and white flowers turned round and looked at Jeremy James, because in the silence his voice came out loud and clear, and Daddy's face went rather red, and he told Jeremy James to keep quiet. And the man in black blew his whistle for a long time, and the players stopped running altogether, and those in red jumped up and down waving their arms, whilst those in blue walked slowly away watching their own feet, and everybody stood up and shouted 'Boo!', as if they wanted to frighten the men on the pitch. And when they'd finished shouting 'Boo!', the people started to shuffle out of the sitting-down stand, and Daddy and Jeremy James shuffled with them, till they were back in the air again, and entering the leg-jungle out in the street, passing cars which were still hooting angrily — in fact doing everything in reverse from when they had come.

'Did you enjoy it, dear?' asked Mummy when they got home.

'Yes thank you,' said Jeremy James, 'it was funny.'

'Who won?' Mummy asked Daddy.

'Hmmph!' said Daddy, 'I must get on with my work,' and he went into his study and closed the door firmly behind him. And he was so quiet that he must have been working very hard indeed.

Uncle Arthur

It was two o'clock in the morning when Uncle Arthur arrived through the window of Jeremy James's bedroom. There was not a sound anywhere in the house, street, town — with the exception of the rumbling, stuttering, pig-snort muttering known as Daddy's Snore to everyone except Daddy, who called it Mummy's Snore. Otherwise it was all very quiet indeed.

Jeremy James, of course, was fast asleep, and would certainly have remained fast asleep if Uncle Arthur hadn't fallen and sat on his head. Having someone sitting on his head was enough to wake even Jeremy James.

Jeremy James didn't know it was Uncle Arthur sitting on his head, because when you've been fast asleep and are woken by being sat on and find that it's pitch dark anyway — well, it's difficult to know who's who and what's what.

So Jeremy James merely sat up in bed (when Uncle Arthur, who at the time was just somebody or the other, had stood up again), and asked who it was. There was a low mumbling noise, which sounded a bit like 'Hmmph', and then complete silence, except for some rather heavy breathing.

'Are you a doggy?' asked Jeremy James.

The doggy didn't reply.

Jeremy James reached out and switched on the light —

for he had a switch right by his bed, in case he felt like wee-weeing in the night.

When he had blinked a few times, he found himself looking at a rather funny little man dressed in a thick sweater and carrying a large sack.

'Hello,' said Jeremy James.

'Hello,' said the funny little man with the sweater and the sack.

'Who are you?' asked Jeremy James.

'Um. . . guess!' said the little man.

'Well, I know Father Christmas carries a sack like that,' said Jeremy James, 'but. . . well, it's not Christmas, and anyway Father Christmas has a long white beard, and you haven't. And Father Christmas isn't bald, and he doesn't wear glasses either. So you're not Father Christmas.'

'No,' said the little man, 'I'm not.'

'And you're not the chimney-sweep,' said Jeremy James.

'Oh!' said the little man, 'what makes you say that?'

'Well for one thing you're not covered in black, and for another, we haven't got any fire-places, and chimney-sweeps have to have fire-places to sweep up, like we had in our last house. And you don't smell. At least, not much.'

'No, I'm not the chimney-sweep,' said the little man.

'Well who are you, then?'

'Ah!' said the little man, looking round the room. 'Ah!'

'R.? R. what?'

'I'm. . . um. . . I'm your Uncle Arthur,' said the little man. 'That's who I am. Your dear old Uncle Arthur.'

'Oh!' said Jeremy James. 'I didn't know I had an Uncle Arthur.'

'No, well, you have now,' said Uncle Arthur. 'But. . . er . . . I think perhaps I'd better slip out again, and come back another time — seeing that it's so late.'

'Oh no,' said Jeremy James, 'I'll tell Mummy and Daddy you're here. I don't think they know I've got an Uncle Arthur either.'

'No, no, I wouldn't do that, son, if I were you. Don't wake them up. I'll. . . I'll come back.'

'It's no trouble,' said Jeremy James, already out of bed, heading for the door, and seeing a pile of pocket-money and ice-cream such as all grateful uncles are obliged to provide for little boys who do them favours.

'Wait, wait!' said Uncle Arthur. 'Wait!'

Jeremy James waited.

'Look. . .' said Uncle Arthur, 'um. . . look. . . your Mummy and Daddy aren't expecting me, you see. They don't know I'm coming. And actually. . . well. . . I don't want them to know I'm here, you see. It's. . . er. . . a secret.'

'A secret?'

'Yes, a secret.'

'You mean like Mummy's new dress which I mustn't tell Daddy about?'

'That's right, yes, just like Mummy's new dress!'

'Good,' said Jeremy James. Mummy's secret was worth tenpence, and uncles are always more generous than mothers. 'I like uncles,' said Jeremy James, 'because uncles always give me things, and Mummy gave me tenpence not to tell Daddy about her new dress.'

'Ah,' said Uncle Arthur. 'Well, if you'll keep this little secret, Johnnie my lad. . .'

'My name's not Johnnie! I'm Jeremy James.'

'Of course, Jeremy James. . . now, if you'll keep this little secret, I'll give you twenty pence. How's that?'

It's wonderful, said Jeremy James to himself. What is it that makes uncles so much more understanding than mothers — and aunts, if it comes to that? They seem to have a better sense of justice. It would be a better world if all aunts and mothers turned into uncles – and that's a fact.

'All right,' said Jeremy James.

'Here,' said Uncle Arthur, reaching into his pocket, and the money was absolutely real, and absolutely right. Twenty pence, in two shining coins.

'And now,' said Uncle Arthur, 'I'll have to be going. I've got a train to catch.'

'Aren't you coming back?' asked Jeremy James.

'Well, not for a while,' said Uncle Arthur. 'I'm a very busy man.'

'I hope you'll come back soon,' said Jeremy James. 'I like uncles.'

Uncle Arthur turned towards the window, which was wide open. Jeremy James walked to the window himself, and saw a ladder leaning on the wall outside.

'Oh, you don't need to go out of the window,' said Jeremy James. 'I know how to open the front door. Come on.'

'No, no,' said Uncle Arthur, 'I always use the window. It's . . . um . . . more fun.'

Jeremy James nodded, as if he agreed. After all, twenty pence is twenty pence.

'Shall I pass your bag out to you?' asked Jeremy James, feeling it was the least he could do.

'Oh, thanks very much, Johnnie.'

'Jeremy James.'

'Jeremy James.'

But the bag turned out to be rather heavy, so Uncle Arthur had to climb back in again after all to get it. And in climbing back in, he scraped his leg on the window-sill and said a word Daddy had used once when he dropped a hammer on his toe.

'Mummy says that's a naughty word,' said Jeremy James.

But Uncle Arthur used the same word again, which confirmed what Jeremy James had already long suspected: Mummy didn't really know what words were naughty and what weren't.

Uncle Arthur grabbed his bag, and climbed out of the window again.

'Goodnight, Uncle Arthur!' shouted Jeremy James, when Uncle Arthur had reached the bottom of the ladder.

Uncle Arthur looked up sharply, as if he wasn't too pleased, whispered goodnight, and ran rather fast out into the darkness of the back garden, so that Jeremy James couldn't see him any more.

33

'Mummy,' said Jeremy James at breakfast next morning. 'When's Uncle Arthur going to come and see us again?'

'Uncle Arthur?' said Mummy. 'You haven't got an Uncle Arthur.'

'Yes I have,' said Jeremy James. 'You know, the bald one who carries a sack.'

'Eat your cornflakes,' said Mummy, 'and don't talk nonsense.'

'He's the one who always comes in through the window.'

'Stop talking, and get on with your cornflakes. You haven't got an Uncle Arthur. Finish.'

Grown-ups really do live in a different world.

Jeremy James Feeds an Elephant

It was one of those bright blue-sky birdsong days when Mummy suddenly remembered that fresh air was good for you and the family hadn't been out for days weeks and months.

'Let's go to the zoo,' she said. Jeremy James smiled.

'What, today?' said Daddy. Jeremy James frowned.

'Yes, today,' said Mummy. 'We could do with some fresh air, and anyway we haven't been out for days weeks months.'

'But it's Saturday,' said Daddy.

'I know,' said Mummy.

'Well . . . the place'll be crowded, and I mean . . .'

'I suppose there's a football match on the television,' said Mummy.

'Well, yes, as it happens there is, but . . .'

And so Mummy, Daddy, and Jeremy James went to the zoo. Jeremy James loved the zoo, and most of the time Mummy and Daddy behaved quite well when they went to the zoo, probably because they liked it too. The only trouble was, they all liked different things. Daddy would settle down in front of the lions' cage and start talking about noble beasts in captivity, or something, and they would have to drag him away or he'd stay there till sleeping-time. Mummy was fascinated by the birds with their bright feathers, and would start talking about colourful nature, patterns, grace, or something like that, and then *she* had to be dragged away. But what annoyed Jeremy James most was that both Mummy and Daddy loved the monkeys, and whilst he and Mummy could drag Daddy away from the lions, and he and Daddy could drag Mummy away from the birds, he all on his own hadn't got a chance of dragging both Mummy and Daddy away from the monkeys.

Today, Mummy and Daddy were extra keen on the monkeys.

'Look at that!' shrieked Mummy, as an ugly creature with a sore bottom jumped on to a rubber tyre and grinned.

'They're a scream,' said Daddy.

But they weren't a scream at all. The fact was that they didn't do anything that Jeremy James couldn't do just as well, but when the monkeys did it, Mummy and Daddy laughed and thought it was wonderful, and when Jeremy James did it, he simply got told off. Only that very morning he had done a magnificent leap from the sofa on to Daddy's armchair – not to mention braving the raging river a thousand feet below – and had merely been drily told not to jump on the furniture. Not a laugh, not a clap . . . just 'Don't jump on the furniture'. And when he swung from the apple tree, did they gaze at him with love and admiration in their eyes? No. Either they didn't watch him at all, or if they did, they simply shouted 'Mind the apples, Jeremy James!' or 'If you tear your trousers, you'll see what you get!' And as for bananas, that was the unfairest cheat of all. They *gave* bananas to the monkeys, just to see how they peeled them, and when the monkeys peeled their bananas, Mummy and Daddy would grin to each other and say how clever the monkeys were. But if Jeremy James asked for a banana (which he could peel a hundred times quicker than any old monkey), they'd say 'Wait till tea-time,' and that was that.

Mummy and Daddy had got stuck in front of the monkeys. They would be there all day, and that was a fact, and Jeremy James couldn't see the joke or the point. So Jeremy James waited till one of the monkeys was being particularly clever (beating his chest and showing his teeth, which was apparently a marvellous trick that had all the grown-ups roaring with laughter), and slipped away into the crowd and off in the direction of the elephant house. Elephants, after all, were the biggest animals, and they were easily the most interesting. Elephants could do things that Jeremy James couldn't do at all. Like squirting water over themselves, picking up buns with their noses, and squashing cars. Elephants were really talented — not like monkeys.

There were lots of people at the elephant house, which wasn't a house at all, but a great big sort of playground with rails round it and with a ditch on the other side of the rails. The elephants could just about reach the rail with their trunks, and sniff up the buns and things people were giving them. Daddy never let Jeremy James feed any animals, because he said there were notices everywhere with 'Don't Feed The Animals' on them — but Daddy was the only one who ever saw these notices, and it was obvious that even if there *were* notices, the animals couldn't have written them, so they were unfair. *Everyone* likes buns and sweets and biscuits and things, and the animals liked them too, so Daddy was probably being mean.

In his pocket, Jeremy James had two slices of bread. He'd smuggled them out of the house. They weren't ordinary bread. They were bread with currants in. The sort of bread elephants dream about. And he'd brought them

37

just for the elephants, and although he'd have liked a bite or two himself — especially of a curranty bit — he could see the expression on the elephant's face already, and he knew the elephant knew the currant bread was for *him*. So Jeremy James didn't take a single bite — not even to taste it.

'Here!' said Jeremy James, and reached out both slices at once. And then the elephant made a very silly mistake. He *took* both slices (with a scrapy, creepy, snuffly whiff of Jeremy James's hand), but between hand and mouth, very foolishly, he forgot there were two. One he tossed into his mouth, and the other he let fall right on the edge of the ditch.

'Hey!' said Jeremy James, 'don't forget the other one!'

But the elephant, who must have been a very stupid elephant, not only forgot it, but also ignored Jeremy James completely. He just turned his head away and looked round for someone else to feed him. And Jeremy James's second slice of currant bread lay all uneaten on the edge of the ditch.

'There, look!' shouted Jeremy James.

'On the edge of the ditch, look!' shouted Jeremy James.

'Opposite your foot!' shouted Jeremy James.

The elephant nearly trod on it, but still didn't see it. Jeremy James remembered one of Daddy's words:

'It's opposite your blooming foot!' he shouted, but the elephant didn't take any notice.

There was only one thing Jeremy James could do. After all, a slice of currant bread is a slice of currant bread, and you don't smuggle currant bread out of the house just to leave it lying on the edge of a ditch. 'You're a stupid elephant,' said Jeremy James, as he slipped be-

tween the railings. 'You're as stupid as those monkeys.'

Jeremy James reached the edge of the ditch, and a great shout went up from the crowd behind as he picked up the slice of currant bread. Then everything seemed to go very quiet indeed. So quiet that Jeremy James turned round to see what was wrong, but all the people were still there — they were just quiet, that was all.

'Here!' said Jeremy James, holding out the currant bread. 'Come on, you stupid elephant!' said Jeremy James.

The elephant slowly turned his head, at last spotted the currant bread, and scrapy-creepy-snuffle-whiffed it out of Jeremy James's hand.

'And about time too!' said Jeremy James. Then he turned round, and squeezed back through the railings, straight into the grip of a man wearing a zoo-keeper uniform, a moustache, and a red face.

'Where's your mother and father?' said the moustache.

'I expect they're still wasting their time watching those monkeys,' said Jeremy James.

But just at that moment Mummy and Daddy arrived, and their faces looked rather red too, and when they saw Jeremy James they both said at the same time, 'Where have you been?' And then the moustache said something to them, and then Daddy said something to the moustache, and then the moustache said something to Daddy which made Daddy's face go very red, and then Daddy said something to Mummy, and Mummy — rather roughly — jerked Jeremy James's arm and led him away from the elephant house, leaving Daddy and the moustache talking together in loud voices.

'You must never,' said Mummy, 'never never never go through fences or try and touch the animals. You understand? They're very very dangerous. You could have been killed!'

'Well I was only giving him a piece of bread he'd dropped,' said Jeremy James, 'and if he hadn't been such a stupid elephant, I wouldn't have had to get it for him.'

But there wasn't really much point in trying to explain it to Mummy, because she didn't have much clue about animals. Someone who prefers monkeys to elephants can't be expected to understand elephants — or little boys, if it comes to that.

Buried Treasure

At the bottom of the garden, right next to the fence that was so tall nobody could ever know what was on the other side, was a patch of land that belonged exclusively to Jeremy James. It wasn't a very big patch of land — because it wasn't a very big garden — but it was by far the most interesting place Jeremy James knew. And when the weather was fine he would often sit down on the ground and watch the ants collecting bits of insect, or the worms wriggling down into the earth, or the flies washing their hands, and he would wish that he was as tiny as they were so that he could recognize their faces and talk to them.

Mummy did give him some seeds once to plant, but nothing ever came of them, and the only thing that flourished on Jeremy James's land was what Daddy used to call flowers, and Mummy called weeds. Mummy said they should be torn up and thrown away, but Jeremy James thought they looked very nice, and as it was *his* patch of land, he was allowed to keep them. Daddy thought he should keep them, too, because he said that 'Jeremy James doesn't have to learn to weed at his age.'

Now the night before the day we're talking about, Mummy had read Jeremy James a very exciting story about pirates, who used to rob people and then bury their treasure deep in the ground where nobody else could find it. (Daddy said they weren't called pirates any more, but tacksinspectus, or some funny name like that.) Jeremy James liked that story very much, and he reckoned that if there had been any pirates around where he lived, there was only one place they could possibly have chosen to bury their treasure and that was the most interesting place he knew. And so next day — and next day is the day that we're talking about — he picked up his seaside spade and marched off to the bottom of the garden in search of fame and fortune.

The earth there wasn't quite as soft as the sand beside the sea, but pirates are clever people and don't bury their treasure where it's easy to find. Jeremy James knew that the harder it was, the more treasure there would be, and so he dug, and dug, and dug, and dug, until his arms and legs began to send complaints up to his head. Fouf, that's enough, they said, we arms and legs could do with a rest and a nice helping of strawberries and ice-cream and fizzy lemonade and a bar of chocolate and a . . . but treasure-hunters' heads never take any notice of their arms and legs.

And just at the moment when the arms and legs were about to refuse to do any more digging for ever and ever, Jeremy James's seaside spade struck something very hard indeed.

'Gosh!' said Jeremy James, and brought his spade down on it again. It felt even harder the second time than the first. Jeremy James got down on his hands and knees, which had stopped sending complaints now, and scraped the earth off the treasure-chest. It was certainly metal, and it was so hard the pirates must have put all the *best* jewels in it.

'Gosh!' said Jeremy James again, and started to dig all around the treasure-chest, because he knew that even the biggest treasure in the world won't buy you many ice-

creams unless you can get it out of the ground. And so
he dug, and then he pulled, and then he pushed, and then
he heaved, and he huffed and he puffed, and he growled
and he howled, and he hugged and he tugged, and he
clasped and he gasped, and he sneezed and he wheezed
. . . but the treasure-chest stayed exactly where it was,
and never moved an inch.

Jeremy James sat down beside the treasure-chest to
have a good think. That was what Daddy always said —
if you have a problem you should sit down and think
about it. Mummy always said if you had a problem you
should get up and do something about it, but Daddy said
Mummy didn't understand about these things, and so he

44

carried on with his thinking and left Mummy to carry on with her doing. The funny thing was that by the time Daddy had finished his thinking, Mummy had usually finished her doing, and there wasn't much of a problem left for Daddy to deal with, but that never seemed to worry Daddy, because he said that only proved how much simpler life was if you sat down and had a good think while someone else was doing the doing.

Anyway, Jeremy James was a man like his Daddy, and so he sat next to his problem and thought about it. There was no way he could get that treasure-chest out of the ground. So what could he do? He could, of course, tell Mummy and Daddy and ask them to help him, but this was *his* land and *his* treasure-chest, and he wanted to show them, not them to show him. He didn't want to ask *anyone* for help. Treasure's treasure, and finding's keepings. But how do you get a treasure out of the ground if it refuses to come? Sometimes Jeremy James refused to come, and Mummy had ways of persuading him, but the treasure-chest hadn't got ears to listen to a telling-off, and it hadn't got a bottom to feel a hard smack, so Mummy's methods certainly wouldn't work.

And then Jeremy James remembered something that had happened a long time ago. Picnic-time out in the green fields, with Daddy talking about the beauty of Nature and Mummy flapping a cloth at the flies and Jeremy James wishing they'd hurry up and bring out the ice-cream. A tin of mandarin oranges, that's what Jeremy James was remembering now. A large tin for once, with a black label and a mouth-watering picture of mandarin oranges right in the middle. And Daddy saying, 'Just what I feel like — some nice juicy mandarin oranges — perfect end to a perfect meal. Eh, Jeremy James? How about some nice juicy mandarin oranges?' and Mummy saying,

'I forgot the tin-opener.' What happened then? Daddy said a few words, and Mummy said she was sorry, and then Daddy sat down to think, and what did Mummy do? She got a knife out of the bag, held the tin very firmly on the ground, and pushed the point of the knife right through the top of the tin. Then she waggled it around until there was a hole big enough for all that sweet, cool, juicy treasure to come pouring out. That was the way to do it. Get something with a sharp point, waggle it around, and out would come all the sparkling gold and silver.

Jeremy James looked down the garden towards the living-room window, the kitchen window, the bedroom window, the bathroom window. Not a Mummy or a Daddy in sight. A quick dash across the lawn, and he was safe inside Daddy's tool-shed. And inside Daddy's tool-shed he soon found just what he was looking for. It was a lot bigger than a knife, and it had a great big handle and a big round pointed head, and Jeremy James could hardly lift it, it was so heavy. But one thump with that, and the treasure would be his for sure. Another quick look down the garden, and then Jeremy James wrestled the pick-axe back across the lawn to the earthy cradle of his golden future.

The pick-axe really was very heavy, but Jeremy James was very determined, and a determined boy and a heavy pick-axe can do quite a lot of damage to a stubborn, stick-in-the-mud treasure-chest. There was a loud clang as pick-axe and treasure-chest were introduced to each other, and Jeremy James bent down to have a look. He hadn't managed to break through yet, but there was a nice deep dent in the metal – and after all, pirates don't bury their gold and silver in mandarin orange tins. One more thump on the same place should do it. The pick-axe wobbled up into the air again, and crashed down

46

into the earth beside the treasure-chest, giving one wriggling pink worm a terrible shock that sent it squirming in all directions at once. 'Missed!' said Jeremy James, and gathered strength for another attack. Three times the pick-axe rose and fell, and by the third stroke there wasn't a worm in sight, but Jeremy James was not to be put off. He took very very careful aim, drew in enough air to float half-a-dozen Christmas balloons, and heaved the pick-axe up to the sky once more. When it came down, there was a glorious crunch as the point pierced the metal, and then a very strange thing happened. There was a great whoosh, and something shot high into the air, and when it came down again it was very wet, and Jeremy James found himself being drenched with the

coldest, heaviest shower he'd ever been showered with.

'Mummy!' he shouted, and dripped hastily across the lawn to the French doors, which opened even before he could shout 'Mummy!' again.

Ever such a lot of things happened during the next hour or so. There were phone calls and runnings backwards and forwards, and The Men came, and Jeremy James was sent to his room, and Daddy had a talk with a big man who had a red face and a bristly moustache, and some of the neighbours knocked on the front door, and The Men kept tramping in and out, and when Jeremy James went to the lavatory it wouldn't flush, and when he told Mummy the lavatory wouldn't flush she smacked his bottom and told him to go back to his room, and in the end, when everyone had gone, the garden looked like a paddling-pool and the house was full of muddy boot-marks which Mummy said were Jeremy James's fault, though the feet were obviously a hundred times bigger than his. And Daddy came upstairs, and sat with Jeremy James on the bed, and put on a very serious, very Daddy-like voice, and told him that he must never, never take the pick-axe again, or go digging again, or go 'messing up the whole caboodle again' — which was very unfair since Jeremy James didn't even know what a caboodle was. And Mummy said he should go to bed without any supper, but Daddy brought him a sandwich and said he'd jolly well better not make any crumbs. And goodnight and God bless.

Jeremy James sat up in bed and munched his sandwich (which was strawberry jam — his favourite) and reflected on the injustices of the world he lived in. Of course, all that water must have caused a lot of trouble, but he'd got as wet as anybody, and it shouldn't have needed much common sense for them to realize that it wasn't his fault. After all, they'd have been pleased enough if he'd come in with his pockets full of gold and silver. Why on earth should they blame him if those stupid pirates had gone and buried a box of water instead?

Jeremy James and the Doctor

Jeremy James wasn't very well. In the night he'd had to call for Mummy, and he'd been very sick — horrible smelly sick, all over the bed-clothes. And Mummy had had to stroke his hair, and sit by him for a while, which was rather nice. And the crispy clean sheets were rather nice, too. But being ill wasn't so nice, especially the being sick part, which was very un-nice. Even Daddy had come in for a few minutes while Jeremy James was being sick — and it took a lot to get Daddy out of bed for *anything* — but Mummy said he looked even worse than Jeremy James felt, so he should go back to bed. And Daddy said something like 'Worple doctor semantics', and Mummy said 'In the morning', and Daddy said 'Semantics doctor worple', and Jeremy James said 'Gloop!' and Daddy went away very quickly and Mummy stayed with Jeremy James.

Now that it was morning, Jeremy James felt a bit better. He didn't feel all better, but just sort of better better. He felt better enough to get up and play, but not better enough to eat his cornflakes and drink his milk. Anyway, Mummy said he wasn't better enough to get up and play either, so he stayed in bed and Mummy phoned for the doctor. When Mummy came back from phoning, she was holding a little packet in her hand. It was a cardboard packet, with lots of bright colours on it, and Jeremy James knew, even before Mummy said anything, just which packet it was and where Mummy had found it.

'Now then,' said Mummy . . . and this wasn't Mummy's are-you-feeling-better-darling voice at all. . . 'last night, Jeremy James, when I changed your pillow, I found this. And it's empty.'

'Yes,' said Jeremy James.

'A quarter of a pound of liquorice-all-sorts,' said Mummy.

'Er . . . hmmph!' said Jeremy James.

'I suppose you ate them all,' said Mummy.

'Oh yes,' said Jeremy James. 'Nobody helped me.'

'After you'd cleaned your teeth,' said Mummy.

'Hmmph!' said Jeremy James.

'And then,' said Mummy, 'you were sick.'

'Well no,' said Jeremy James, 'I wasn't sick *then*. I wasn't, Mummy, not *then*.'

'Oh?' said Mummy.

'I didn't feel at all sick *then*. I went to sleep, that's what I did *then*.'

'Jeremy James,' said Mummy, 'you must never, never eat sweets before you go to sleep. You must never eat anything after you've cleaned your teeth. And you must never, never, never eat a whole box of liquorice-all-sorts at one go. Do you hear?'

'Yes, Mummy,' said Jeremy James.

'One liquorice-all-sort, or maybe two,' said Mummy, 'and that's enough.'

'Yes, Mummy,' said Jeremy James, though inside he said to himself that one liquorice-all-sort, or maybe two, wasn't enough and never could be enough, and only a grown-up would ever imagine that it *was* enough, because only grown-ups liked little helpings of nice things and big helpings of nasty things. Mummy would never say, for instance, 'One potato, or maybe two, and that's enough', or one cornflake, or one carrot, or one cabbage leaf. Oh no, you could have as many of those things as you liked (or didn't like). But ask for more mandarin oranges, more chocolate, more liquorice-all-sorts, and all you'd get was the no-more-they're-not-good-for-you gramophone record.

Dr Bassett was the tallest man in the world. He was taller than the house, because when he came into Jeremy James's room, he had to bend down so that his head wouldn't go through the roof. He was taller than the apple tree, because the apple tree wasn't as tall as the house, and so he must have been taller than Daddy, because Daddy couldn't reach the top of the apple tree, except when he borrowed Mr. Robertson's ladder, and even then he usually couldn't get to the top of the apple tree because either he or the ladder kept falling down. Dr Bassett was a very tall man.

'Well now, old chap,' said Dr Bassett, 'how are we feeling?'

'Who?' said Jeremy James.

'You,' said Dr Bassett.

'Oh,' said Jeremy James. 'I'm very well, thank you, and I've been sick.'

'Ah,' said Dr Bassett.

'He ate a quarter of a pound of liquorice-all-sorts before he went to bed,' said Mummy.

'It wasn't before I went to bed,' said Jeremy James, 'it was after I went to bed.'

'Ah,' said Dr Bassett, 'that does make a difference.'

Dr Bassett had a very interesting-looking black bag, which was full of chocolate, tins of fruit, toy soldiers, toy guns and railway engines, until he opened it, and

then it was full of very boring things like youknowwhats and whatdoyoucallits. Jeremy James was poked with a youknowwhat, and pulled a face, then he was tickled with a whatdoyoucallit, and giggled. Then Dr Bassett looked into his mouth, felt his head, tapped his chest and ruffled his hair.

'He'll be all right,' said Dr Bassett.

'No I won't,' said Jeremy James. 'Because I'm not ill where you were looking and you were looking in the wrong place.'

'Ah,' said Dr Bassett.

'Jeremy James!' said Mummy.

'And where should I have looked?' said Dr Bassett.

'In my tummy,' said Jeremy James. 'That's where I'm ill, 'cos that's where the pain was.'

'Of course,' said Dr Bassett. 'Aren't I a silly old doctor, not looking in your tummy? Let's have a look at it then.'

And Dr Bassett had a very close look at Jeremy James's tummy. He bent right over like the beanstalk must have done when Jack chopped it, and Jeremy James could see through his grey hair and on to his shiny head, and Dr Bassett pointed his little torch on to Jeremy James's tummy, and studied the tummy for a very long time.

'Well,' said Dr Bassett, 'you were quite right, Jeremy James. There's a pink liquorice-all-sort in there, and it's been having a fight with a blue liquorice-all-sort, and that's what all the trouble was about. If you'd just eaten a blue liquorice-all-sort, or you'd just eaten a pink one, they couldn't have had a fight, and you wouldn't have been ill. It's a good thing you told me to look, isn't it?'

'Yes,' said Jeremy James.

'Anyway,' said Dr Bassett, turning to Mummy, 'he's got a little bit of a temperature. It's probably a touch of flu, as a matter of fact. I should keep him in bed for a day or two, and just give him plenty of liquids. He'll soon let you know himself when he's better. I'll write you out a prescription. . .'

Now this was all very strange. Because Dr Bassett had been to the house before. And the last time Dr Bassett had come to the house, it hadn't been to see Jeremy James, but to see Daddy because Daddy had been dying, and dying very loudly, with a lot of 'foofs' and 'phaws' and 'hmmphs' and 'aaahs'. And Dr Bassett had Jack-and-the-beanstalked over Daddy, too, and poked him and tickled him, and Daddy had said something about it being the end, and Dr Bassett had said it wasn't quite

the end, but it was . . . it definitely was . . . it most certainly was . . . a touch of flu. And if Daddy had a touch of flu then, and Jeremy James had a touch of flu now . . . It was all very complicated, but Jeremy James managed to work it out just before Dr Bassett folded himself in two to get through the door.

'Excuse me,' said Jeremy James, because that was what you always said to grown-ups when you wanted them to turn and look at you.

'Yes, old chap?' said Dr Bassett, turning to look at Jeremy James.

'Can you,' said Jeremy James, 'get a touch of flu through eating too many liquorice-all-sorts?'

'Ah,' said Dr Bassett. 'I'll have to ask the Royal Society to look into that one. But as far as I know, most people find a different way of getting it.'

'Well, did my Daddy get it through eating too many liquorice-all-sorts?' said Jeremy James.

Dr Bassett seven-league-booted back to the bed, and whispered very, very secretly: 'That's highly problematical. You see, it's only very clever people that get a touch of flu through eating too many liquorice-all-sorts. Now, do you think that's how you got yours?'

Jeremy James had a quick think, because you have to have a quick think before you answer a question like that.

'Well,' said Jeremy James, 'I think that maybe I possibly might have done.'

'I think you possibly might have done as well,' said Dr Bassett.

And Jeremy James sat back in his bed and tried to work out whether it was better to be clever and eat liquorice-all-sorts and get a touch of flu, or not to be clever and not to eat liquorice-all-sorts and not to get a touch of flu. The best thing might be to be clever and to eat liquorice-all-sorts and not to get a touch of flu, but Dr Bassett had already gone, and it was too late to ask him whether anyone possibly might have been clever enough to do that.

Timothy

Timothy lived next door, and he was Jeremy James's best friend, and Jeremy James didn't like him very much. The trouble with Timothy was that he was spoilt, and anything Jeremy James had, Timothy had too but even more so. If Jeremy James had a train set to go round the living-room, Timothy had a train set to go round the living-room *and* the dining-room *and* the hall. If Jeremy James had a tricycle with a bell, Timothy had a tricycle with a bell *and* a hooter *and* a saddle-bag. And if Jeremy James went to the zoo on a Saturday, Timothy had already been there on Friday, which was the only day when elephants were allowed to escape and little boys were allowed to ride on them.

Timothy was one year older than Jeremy James, and he was taller, fatter, stronger, richer. Timothy had red hair, and told Jeremy James over and over again that red hair was the best thing anyone could have on top of his head. Timothy had freckles on his face, and as everyone knows, a face without freckles can hardly be called a face. But worst of all, Timothy went to school, and any-one who hasn't been to school simply doesn't know what life is all about. Timothy did all kinds of marvellous things at school, like eating all day long, teaching the teachers how to do reading and writing, making pictures which were the best pictures anyone had ever made

before because his Daddy said so, and fighting ten boys
at a time and knocking them all out with a single punch.
Timothy knew everything, could do everything, had
done everything.

Timothy had a great big tent in which he and Jeremy
James could play Indians. Jeremy James had a tent, too,
but there was only room for one Indian in his tent.
Timothy's tent could hold a tribe. And so they always
played Indians in Timothy's tent in Timothy's garden,
which was bigger than Jeremy James's garden. Timothy
was always the chief — after all, it was *his* tent and *his*
garden — and Jeremy James was either a miserable
Indian tied to a stake ready for painful torture and

eventual head-cutting-off, or he was a miserable cowboy awaiting the same fate. The only time Jeremy James was allowed to torture and cut off heads was if Billy Wilkinson from over the road came and played with them, or his baby sister Gillian, but they were so small that you couldn't really enjoy cutting their heads off because it was too easy, and anyway they didn't know you were doing it, and as they didn't know, they didn't scream, and cutting heads off without screaming is like eating strawberries without any cream.

Now the first Sunday after Jeremy James had been in bed with liquorice-all-sort flu, he and Timothy were out in Timothy's tent, and Jeremy James had just had his head cut off for the twentieth time.

'Can I cut your head off now?' said Jeremy James.

'No,' said Timothy. 'It's my tent.'

'It's not fair,' said Jeremy James for the twenty-first time.

'And it's my garden, too,' said Timothy.

'Well let's go and play in my tent in my garden,' said Jeremy James.

'Your tent's too small,' said Timothy, 'and if we don't play here then I'm not playing at all. And I'm older than you and I'm bigger than you.'

All of which was very true.

'Well I've had flu,' said Jeremy James, which was also true, but didn't really have a great deal to do with the question under discussion.

'I know,' said Timothy. 'I had flu when I was your age, but I've grown out of it now.'

'You can't grow out of flu,' said Jeremy James, ' 'cos my Daddy's had it — the doctor said.'

'I know,' said Timothy, 'but that's different — the flu that grown-ups get can't be grown out of. I learnt all about it at school. There's grown-up flu, and other flu.'

'Well I had the same as Daddy,' said Jeremy James.

'You didn't,' said Timothy.

'I did,' said Jeremy James.

And after five minutes of I-did-you-didn'ting, Timothy jumped on Jeremy James and cut off his head for the twenty-first time and as far as he was concerned, that proved that Jeremy James didn't have grown-up flu.

Now Jeremy James was certainly smaller than Timothy, and younger, and not so richly endowed with experience of the great big world outside, but Jeremy James was also very determined and in his own way extremely clever. And what was even more important — he was right, and Timothy was wrong. So when the Great Apache Chief had got off his victim and lowered his bloodstained tomahawk, Jeremy James scrambled to his feet and informed his tormentor that not only was he, Jeremy James, right, but also he, Timothy, was wrong, and he, Jeremy James could prove that he, Timothy, had not grown out of flu at all but could be given the *same* flu as he, Jeremy James, had so recently fought and conquered. The *same*. And he, Jeremy James, could prove it.

'You can't,' said Timothy.

'I can,' said Jeremy James. ' 'Cos I know what I got it from — I got it from a special medicine, and you'll get the same flu if you take the medicine, so there.'

'I won't,' said Timothy.

'You will,' said Jeremy James.

'Prove it,' said Timothy.

At this moment, Jeremy James had a vague feeling that he should have reached for his six-shooter and shot Timothy through the chest, but he hadn't got his six-shooter with him.

'Wait here,' he said, leapt on his horse, and galloped at breakneck speed through the fence, across the lawn, through the back door, through the living-room, up the stairs, and into his own bedroom. And there, in a very very secret place which no one must ever mention on pain of having his head cut off, Jeremy James uncovered his treasure-chest and, from the pile of biscuits, cakes, sweets and chocolate which no one must ever mention on pain of being tied to a stake and tortured to death, he extracted a large brightly coloured box. Then he put his treasure-chest back in the very very secret place, leapt on to his horse, and galloped at breakneck speed out of his bedroom, down the stairs, through the living-room, through the back door, across the lawn, through the fence, and into Timothy's tent.

'Here,' said Jeremy James. 'Flu medicine.'

'I know what those are,' said Timothy. 'They're liquorice-all-sorts.'

'They may look like liquorice-all-sorts,' said Jeremy James, 'but they're really flu medicine, and you've got to eat them all, and you'll get flu just like the flu I had and Daddy had and it's the *same* flu.'

'You can't get flu from liquorice-all-sorts,' said Timothy.

'Oh yes you can,' said Jeremy James, ' 'cos the doctor said so, but you just have to be clever to get it, that's all, and maybe you're not clever enough.'

Now Timothy knew you couldn't get flu from eating liquorice-all-sorts, because that was just the sort of thing he'd learned at school, but Timothy rather liked liquorice-all-sorts, and it wasn't every day of the week that somebody put a whole box of liquorice-all-sorts in your hand and actually *told* you to eat them, and even though he was a very great Indian chief, and Jeremy

James was only a miserable Indian or a miserable cow-boy, a box of liquorice-all-sorts was a box of liquorice-all-sorts, and this was a very big box of liquorice-all-sorts, and . . . well . . .

'All right,' said Timothy, 'I'll show you.'

And he showed Jeremy James. One after another he gobbled up the flu medicine all-sorts — pink ones, black ones, blue ones, stripy ones, speckled ones, yellow ones, brown ones, round ones, square ones . . .

'Maybe I should just have one . . .' said Jeremy James.

'No,' said Timothy, 'you gave them to me so they're mine, and anyway it's my tent and my garden.'

Which was true.

And down went the liquorice-all-sorts, and the packet got emptier and emptier, and Timothy's mouth got blacker and blacker, and Jeremy James got hungrier and hungrier.

'There you are,' said Timothy, 'all gone. And I haven't got flu, you see. I told you I wouldn't.'

'Hmmph,' said Jeremy James.

Then they buried the packet as if it was a bone, and hurried off obediently in answer to a double Mummy call of 'Tea-time!' Jeremy James hurried considerably more hurriedly than Timothy. In fact Timothy couldn't really be said to have hurried at all — he sort of un-hurried to the house, as if he had something very heavy inside which had slipped down to his feet and made them difficult to lift.

That evening, Mummy spotted Dr Bassett's car from the window.

'That's funny,' said Mummy. 'Someone must be ill next door — I've just seen the doctor go in.'

'I know,' said Jeremy James. 'It's Timothy. He's got flu.'

'How do you know that, dear?' said Mummy.

'Hmmph,' said Jeremy James, and gave a little smile as he beheaded a toy soldier.

The Bathroom Lock

Daddy had been going to mend the bathroom lock straightaway for about two weeks now. Practically every day Mummy had said to him, 'I do wish you'd get that bathroom lock fixed, dear,' and Daddy had said, 'I'll do it straightaway — as soon as I've finished this.' And this, which had also been that, those and the others, always kept Daddy fully occupied until lunch, tea, supper, or bed-time. Thus the bathroom lock remained well and truly unmended, and every morning, when Jeremy James went to do his Number Two, Mummy had to say to him, 'Don't lock the bathroom door, Jeremy James,' and Jeremy James would say, 'Why not?' and Mummy would say, 'Because it hasn't been mended yet,' and Daddy would say, 'I'll get that seen to straightaway — as soon as I've finished this.'

But one morning, Mummy forgot to say to Jeremy James, 'Don't lock the bathroom door, Jeremy James,' and Jeremy James locked it. As soon as he'd locked it, he remembered that he shouldn't have locked it, and he waited for the house to fall down, but it didn't, and so he sat down to do his Number Two, and wondered what all the fuss had been about.

'Hurry up in there,' said Mummy, when Jeremy James had only been sitting there for a quarter of a minute.

'I'm doing my Number Two!' said Jeremy James. These things can't always be hurried.

However, this morning was a nice sunny morning, which should be good for swinging and tricycling and — with a bit of luck — cowboys-and-indianing in Timothy's tent next door, and so Jeremy James quickly broke the world record for sheets of toilet paper, washed his hands with the nice-smelling soap that nobody but Mummy was allowed to use, and pulled open the bathroom door. That is to say, he pulled the bathroom door to what should have been open, but the bathroom door had other ideas and stayed shut. 'Ah,' said Jeremy James, 'it's locked, that's why,' and so he turned the key. That is to say, he pulled the key to what should have been a turn, but the key only went halfway round and then refused to move another inch. 'Come on, key,' said Jeremy James, but the key wouldn't come on, round, or out. It simply stayed where it was — like the Grand Old Duke of York's Men, neither up nor down.

'Mummy,' said Jeremy James. 'Mummy! Mummy!'

'Did you call, Jeremy James?'

'I'm stuck in the bathroom!'

Silence. Thump, thump, up the stairs. Creak, creak, as Mummy pushes the bathroom door, and the bathroom door pushes back.

'You locked it, did you?' says Mummy through the locked door.

'I forgot,' says Jeremy James.

'John!' says Mummy. 'John! John!'

'Did you call, dear?'

'Jeremy James is stuck in the bathroom!'

Silence. Thump, thump, up the stairs. Creak, creak, as Daddy pushes the bathroom door, and the bathroom door pushes back.

'You locked it, did you?' says Daddy through the locked door.

'Of course he locked it,' says Mummy. 'Otherwise he wouldn't be stuck, would he?'

There was a long silence outside the bathroom door. Daddy must have been thinking.

'Is anybody there?' said Jeremy James.

'It's all right,' said Daddy. 'I'm thinking. Now don't worry, we'll soon get you out of there. Don't worry, son. Just keep calm.'

'I was only wondering if anybody was there,' said Jeremy James.

'Now listen,' said Daddy. 'I'm going to pull the door. And when I tell you, I want you to try and turn the key. Do you understand?'

'Yes,' said Jeremy James.

The door creaked.

'Now!' said Daddy. And Jeremy James's hand turned, but the key stayed where it was.

'It's not moving,' said Jeremy James.

'All right,' said Daddy. 'Now don't worry, I'll soon get you out.'

'You'll have to get a ladder,' said Mummy.

'Wait a moment,' said Daddy. 'Jeremy James, can you get the key out of the lock?'

'No,' said Jeremy James.

'Well try,' said Daddy.

Jeremy James tried.

'No,' said Jeremy James.

'You'll have to get a ladder,' said Mummy.

'Now look,' said Daddy. 'I'll pull the door again, and when I tell you, try turning the key *the other way*. You understand? Try and turn it the other way — the way you weren't turning it before.'

'All right,' said Jeremy James.

'Now,' said Daddy.

And Jeremy James's hand turned the other way, but the key stayed where it was.

'It's not moving,' said Jeremy James.

'You'll have to get a ladder,' said Mummy.

'Now don't worry, son,' said Daddy. 'We'll soon get you out. Maybe I'd better go and get a ladder.'

'Mrs. Robertson opposite has got a big ladder. She's usually in at this time.'

'You stay here, then,' said Daddy. 'Keep talking to him — you know, calm him down. Child must be scared stiff. Which are the Robertsons?'

'Number 14, over the road.'

'Is their name Robertson? I thought they were the Wilkinsons.'

'The Wilkinsons are Number 16. Do go and get the ladder, dear.'

'All right, Jeremy James,' said Daddy. 'I'm just going to get a ladder from the Wilkinsons.'

'The Robertsons.'

'. . . the Robertsons, and I'll be back in half a minute. You keep calm, son, we'll soon have you out of there. You're all right, aren't you?'

'Yes, thank you, Daddy.'

'Nothing to worry about.'

And there was a thump thump clatter crash, as Daddy raced down the first dozen stairs and fell down the rest.

'Jeremy James,' said Mummy, 'is the bathroom window open?'

'No,' said Jeremy James, 'it's shut.'

'Do you think you can open it?'

'Yes, I think so,' said Jeremy James. 'I can climb on the bath.'

'Then open it, only be very careful,' said Mummy. 'Mind you don't fall.'

Jeremy James climbed up on to the edge of the bath, and then stepped very carefully across to the other side. He was being very brave. After all, it's not every day you have to step across a cliff that's a thousand foot high, with hundreds of crocodiles waiting down below with great big open jaws and rumbling tummies. Jeremy James balanced on the edge of the bath, and held on to

69

the towel-rail to make sure he didn't turn into crocodile breakfast. Then he reached up, and with a flick of his hero's hand, turned the catch that would save the world.

Through the open window he could peep down into the garden below. It was quite a long way down, and if you fell from there you'd certainly be killed.

'Have you got it open?' said Mummy.

'Yes,' said Jeremy James, 'and it's ever such a long way down to the garden, and if I fell from here I'd be killed.'

'Now you be careful!' said Mummy. 'Keep right away from the window!'

'You keep calm!' said Jeremy James. 'Don't worry, I'll be all right.'

And just then there was a scratchy scrapy sound against the wall as Daddy persuaded the ladder to stand up against it. Then there was a bumpy bouncy sound as the top part of the ladder decided it would rather be with the bottom part of the ladder, and went racing down the wall, just missing Daddy, who had managed to jump aside at the last moment. Daddy then let out one or two of the words Jeremy James must *never never* use, and there was a long silence.

Jeremy James peeped out of the window.

'Daddy's hurt himself,' said Jeremy James.

Mummy thump-thumped down the stairs and out into the garden, and Jeremy James leaned out of the window to look at Mummy looking at Daddy.

'I'll just get you a plaster,' Mummy was saying, and Daddy was saying, 'Blooming ladder . . . death-trap . . . worple worple semantics,' and things like that.

'Are you all right?' said Jeremy James.

'You get back in, and keep away from the window!' said Daddy. 'It's all your fault in the first place!'

'If you'd mended the lock when . . .' Jeremy James missed the rest of what Mummy was saying, because he'd stepped back from the window, forgotten where he was, and gone tumbling a thousand foot down into the watery jaws of the bath-tub. By the time he'd killed twenty crocodiles — which took him at least twenty seconds — the ladder was up the wall and Daddy was up the ladder, his white face peering through the open window.

'Jeremy James, Jeremy James, are you all right?'

Jeremy James finished off the twenty-first crocodile, and scrambled victoriously to his feet. 'Hello, Daddy.'

'Are you all right, son?'

'Yes, thank you.'

With a heave and a grunt and a fouf and a few of those words, Daddy squeezed himself across the window-ledge and down headfirst into the bath, followed by a shower of bottles, toothpaste, sponges and motor boats. Fortunately the crocodiles were all dead by now, or Daddy really would have been in trouble.

'Are you all right, Daddy?' said Jeremy James.

Daddy got his head up where his feet had been, and put his feet down where his head had been, and then gave Jeremy James a funny look. 'Yes,' he said. 'Apart from a broken arm, a broken leg and a broken neck. And how are you?'

'Not too bad, thank you,' said Jeremy James. 'But the crocodiles *nearly* got me.'

'Crocodiles in the bath, eh?' said Daddy.

'But I killed them all in the end.'

'Good,' said Daddy. 'I'm in no condition to fight crocodiles.'

Then Daddy got the bathroom door unlocked, and Mummy gave Jeremy James a big hug and a big kiss and promised him ice-cream for dinner because he'd been so brave, and Jeremy James said it was nothing, and he wouldn't mind being locked in the bathroom every day, and Daddy took the ladder back to the Robertsons, and Mummy gave Jeremy James a sweet, and Daddy came back from the Robertsons, and Mummy said to Daddy, 'Hadn't you better go and mend that lock now?' and Daddy said, 'I'll just get some plaster on this hand,' and Mummy said, 'Hmmph.' But Daddy really did mend the lock as soon as he'd put the plaster on his hand. And when he'd finished mending the lock, he had to put some plaster on the other hand as well. Daddy always used a lot of plaster when he was mending things.

The Baby-sitter

Mummy and Daddy were going out. They were going to what Mummy called a 'do' and Daddy called a 'worple worple nuisance', and it meant that they had to put on very smart clothes, and Daddy would be ready very early and Mummy would be ready very late. So Jeremy James and the baby-sitter sat in the living-room, and Daddy kept walking up and down, looking at his watch, and shouting, 'Come on, dear, we'll be late!' and Mummy kept calling out, 'Just coming!' and didn't come. And then she did come, and Daddy said, 'Don't you look lovely!' and 'That was certainly worth waiting for!' and kissed her. Then he said, 'We'll be late,' and Mummy said, 'The place won't run away,' and she gave Jeremy James a nice kiss and she smelt just like a queen. When Mummy and Daddy went out, they seemed quite different somehow.

While Daddy stood outside the front door, Mummy told the baby-sitter when Jeremy James was to go to bed, what she was to do if he said he wouldn't go to bed, where to find the tea, the biscuits and the cake, how the television worked, what number to phone if the house caught fire, where she had bought that lovely green tablecloth, what time they would be back . . . 'Come on, dear!' said Daddy, from miles away. 'Coming!' said Mummy — and ten minutes later, they were gone.

73

The baby-sitter was rather old — she must have been at least seventeen — and she had black hair and glasses and a soft voice. Jeremy James liked her soft voice, because he couldn't imagine a soft voice like that ever saying, 'Jeremy James, do as you're told!' or 'Jeremy James, put those sweets away this minute!' or 'Jeremy James, you must go to bed immediately!' A soft voice like that would certainly say, 'Um . . . would you mind . . .' and would keep quiet if you said you *would* mind. Jeremy James liked baby-sitters with soft voices.

'Are you sleepy yet?' said the soft voice.

'No,' said Jeremy James, 'but I'm very hungry.'

And the baby-sitter went into the kitchen and came back with a plate of cakes and biscuits which were cakier and biskier than any of the old cakes and biscuits Jeremy James was given for tea.

'Would you like one of these?' said the baby-sitter, and Jeremy James proceeded to like rather more than one of these, and the baby-sitter never said a word.

'Now what would you like to do?' said the baby-sitter, when Jeremy James had finished the cakes and biscuits.

Nobody had ever before asked Jeremy James what he would *like* to do. He'd been told what he ought to like to do, and he'd been told what he had to do, and he'd been told what he shouldn't have done — but what he would *like* to do, that was something quite new. It needed to be thought about very carefully, and so he sat in his chair, licking the chocolate ring round his mouth, and thought about it very carefully. What would he *really* like to do? With the whole world suddenly open to him, with everything allowed, with a choice that was his and his alone . . . what *would* he like to do?

'I'd like to play hide-and-seek,' said Jeremy James,

and the pearly gates of paradise opened before him.
'Hide-and-seek,' he said, '*that's* what I'd like to do.'

'All right,' said the baby-sitter, 'who's going to hide,
you or me?'

'I'll hide,' said Jeremy James, 'and you must close
your eyes and count up to a hundred. And you mustn't
open your eyes, because that's called cheating.'

And so the baby-sitter closed her eyes, and Jeremy
James tiptoed upstairs and crept into Mummy and
Daddy's room and dived into Mummy and Daddy's bed,
which he wasn't ever supposed to dive into, but which it
was all right to dive into now, because he was playing
hide-and-seek with the baby-sitter, and that was official.
And it was lovely and soft and warm in Mummy and
Daddy's bed, even though Mummy and Daddy weren't
in it, and Jeremy James curled up and listened for the
footsteps of the baby-sitter. Thump, thump she came up
the stairs, and Jeremy James giggled because she'd never
think of looking in Mummy and Daddy's bedroom, and
thump thump came the steps, straight into Mummy and
Daddy's bedroom, on went the light, and 'Caught you!'
said the baby-sitter, and 'That's not fair!' said Jeremy
James. 'You cheated! You opened your eyes!' 'I heard
you laughing!' said the baby-sitter. 'Well it's not fair,'
said Jeremy James. 'You weren't supposed to listen.'

But the baby-sitter *had* listened, and the baby-sitter
had caught him, and now, she insisted, it was her turn
to hide and Jeremy James would have to look for her,
and he must close his eyes and count up to a hundred.

'Well I can't,' said Jeremy James, 'I can only count
up to twenty-ten, so there!'

But Jeremy James did close his eyes. Then the baby-
sitter left the room, and Jeremy James opened his eyes
again, because after all if it was fair for her to listen then

it was fair for him to look. So he tiptoed to the door, peeped out, and saw the baby-sitter disappearing into the bathroom.

'Nineteen, twenty, twenty-ten, a hundred,' said Jeremy James, 'and here I come.' And he went straight to the bathroom, opened the door, said 'Caught you!' and then looked for the baby-sitter. But there was no baby-sitter to be seen. 'Oh!' said Jeremy James, and went out of the bathroom. 'That's funny,' said Jeremy James. Then he looked in the bathroom again, but there was still no baby-sitter.

'Where are you?' said Jeremy James.

He had a good look in the bath, but she was definitely not in it, and he had a look in the bathroom stool, but she wasn't in that either. And she wasn't in the airing-cupboard and she wasn't down the lavatory.

'I know where you are,' said Jeremy James, but that didn't make the baby-sitter appear either. 'I don't know where you are,' said Jeremy James. 'Where are you?' said Jeremy James. And then he went out on to the landing, into Mummy and Daddy's room, into his own room, into the guest room, and he opened all the cupboards and all the drawers, and he looked in all the beds, and he looked under all the beds, and he looked behind all the beds . . . but there was still no baby-sitter. And he decided that hide-and-seek really wasn't so much fun after all, and it would be better to play something else, and the baby-sitter was cheating and it only went to prove that you couldn't play proper games with girls, even if they were official girls like the baby-sitter.

'Where are you?' he said. 'Come out, I don't want to play any more, I give up, it's a silly game . . .' etc. etc. and at last the baby-sitter came into view as she stepped out from behind the bathroom door.

'Caught you!' said Jeremy James, but he wasn't really convinced of that himself. 'Anyway, that was a silly place to hide . . . it's not fair to hide there . . . it's my turn . . . you must close your eyes . . .'

'I thought you didn't want to play hide-and-seek any more,' said the baby-sitter.

'Well, just once more,' said Jeremy James. 'I'll hide and you count up to a hundred. And you mustn't open your eyes.'

So the baby-sitter went back into the bathroom and closed her eyes, and Jeremy James padded downstairs, thinking very very hard. This time he'd find a really *good* place to hide, somewhere she'd never *think* of looking, the best hiding-place anyone had ever found in the whole world. But where?

Jeremy James crept into the kitchen. Where?

Jeremy James looked at the kitchen windows. Jeremy James looked at the kitchen door. Jeremy James opened the kitchen door, giggled, stepped out into the twilit garden, and softly closed the kitchen door behind him. Then ever so quietly he tiptoed across the lawn, opened the door to Daddy's tool-shed, squeezed in, and closed the door again. She'd never find him here, and that was a fact. Jeremy James giggled. She could open her eyes now, *and* she could listen if she wanted to — but she wouldn't find him.

Jeremy James curled up in a deck-chair, and pulled an old rug over himself. It wasn't as soft or as warm as Mummy and Daddy's bed, but it was *quite* soft and it was *quite* warm, and it was rather cosy in the tool-shed, and she'd certainly never find him there, and hide-and-seek was a nice game after all, and she wasn't bad company for a girl, and she was a lot better than some of the baby-sitters that had looked after him, and she had a quiet voice, and . . . and . . . and . . . Jeremy James fell fast asleep.

A lot of things happened that night. First of all, Mummy and Daddy came home from the 'do' a lot earlier than expected. They came home because they'd had a phone call from the baby-sitter, who'd sounded very upset and rather frightened. Then there were some policemen who came in a big blue car, and *they* came because *they'd* had a phone call from Daddy, who'd sounded very upset and rather frightened. And some of the neighbours came to the house, because Mummy had knocked on their doors, and Mummy had sounded very upset and rather frightened. But Jeremy James didn't know about all this, because he was fast asleep, minding his own business in Daddy's tool-shed. It wasn't until he was carried into the house in the arms of a great big policeman with a red face and a bristling moustache that Jeremy James began to take notice of all the activity around him, but even then he was very sleepy and couldn't quite make up his mind whether the policeman was real or just part of a funny dream. Then he was passed across to Daddy's arms and he heard Mummy's voice, and he opened his eyes wide because it sounded as if Mummy was crying. And it really was Mummy and she really was crying, and he really was in Daddy's arms, and there really was a great big policeman there, and

lots of other people were there, too, and over in a corner was the baby-sitter, and she looked as if she was crying as well.

'Oh, hello,' said Jeremy James. 'You didn't find me, did you?'

Then the policeman with the red face and bristling moustache said he'd like a word with Daddy, and Daddy said maybe Jeremy James had better go to bed, and so Jeremy James was passed to Mummy, and Mummy carried him up the stairs to his bed, tucked him in, looked at him for a very long time, and then kissed him goodnight.

'Mummy,' said Jeremy James, 'I had ever such a nice time with the baby-sitter. Can she come here again to look after me?'

'Hmmph,' said Mummy. 'Well as a matter of fact, I don't think she *will* be coming again, Jeremy James.'

'Oh Mummy, why not?' said Jeremy James.

'Because . . .' said Mummy, '. . . because she's not very good at hide-and-seek, that's why.'

And Mummy was right because the baby-sitter didn't come again. And Daddy put a lock on the tool-shed, which was something he'd been meaning to do for ages.

A Death in the Family

Great-Aunt Maud was dead. She was Mummy's Great-Aunt Maud, which made her Jeremy James's Great-Great Aunt Maud, but Jeremy James didn't know her anyway, so as far as he was concerned, it didn't matter whether she was Great, Great-Great, or Not-So-Great. What was much more impressive was the fact that she was ninety-two when she died.

'Ninety-two!' said Jeremy James, when he heard the news. 'But that's enormously old! That's hundreds of years old! That's even older than Daddy!'

Mummy held the letter in her hand, and shed a few tears.

'I don't know what you're crying about,' said Daddy. 'We never could stand her. She was a silly old woman.'

'But she's dead,' said Mummy.

'Well then, she's a dead silly old woman,' said Daddy. 'Look at all the trouble she caused before we got married.'

'That's all in the past,' said Mummy. 'And you shouldn't speak ill of the dead.'

'It doesn't hurt the dead as much as it hurts the living,' said Daddy, 'and that's a fact.'

The funeral was on Saturday. Daddy said he would stay at home and look after Jeremy James, but Mummy said he wouldn't and Jeremy James would have to go as well. Then Daddy said he wouldn't go whatever happened, and Mummy said he was being childish, and Daddy said it was a matter of principle, and Mummy said it was a matter of football, and Daddy proved it wasn't a matter of football by saying all right, he'd go, but only under some sort of umbrella called protest. And so on Saturday Jeremy James was suddenly face to face with a Mummy and Daddy who really didn't look like Mummy and Daddy at all. Mummy had on a black hat and a black dress and black stockings and black shoes, and Jeremy James asked her if she was going to sweep chimneys and Mummy said no she wasn't, and Daddy laughed. As for Daddy, he was wearing a dark grey suit, a black tie, and shoes that shone like glass.

'Is that really you, Daddy?' said Jeremy James, and Daddy said he didn't think it was, and Mummy laughed. Then Mummy said they shouldn't be making jokes on a day like today, and Daddy said today was as good as any other day. Then Mummy dressed Jeremy James up in a smart grey suit he didn't even know he had, and off they drove to the funeral.

'You might have cleaned the car,' said Mummy.

'Weren't enough teardrops in the bucket,' said Daddy.

There were a few teardrops at the funeral, though. Melissa, Aunt Janet's little girl, kept stamping her foot and saying she wanted her dolly, and Aunt Janet gave her a big smack on her bottom which brought forth a whole flood of tears, but no dolly. Otherwise it was a very dull funeral, and the man who stood near the hole in the ground reading bits out of a book had the sort of voice that could put even dead people to sleep. The only interesting moment came when they lifted up a big wooden box and lowered it into the hole in the ground. It was a beautiful, shiny box, which looked very heavy and could have held at least a thousand bars of chocolate and two thousand soldiers.

'Daddy,' said Jeremy James, 'what's in that box?'

'Great-Aunt Maud,' said Daddy, and put his fingers on his lips.

'But what's she doing in there?' said Jeremy James.

'Being dead,' said Daddy.

'Well, what will she do when she wakes up?' said Jeremy James. 'Won't she bump her head?'

'She's not going to wake up,' said Daddy.

'Sh!' said Mummy.

'Why not?' said Jeremy James.

'Because she's dead,' said Daddy. 'Now keep quiet.'

'Well,' said Jeremy James, 'if she's not going to wake up, what does she need that box for?'

'That's enough, Jeremy James!' said Mummy, in her that's-enough voice.

Jeremy James would have liked to ask whether perhaps *he* could have the box since Great-Aunt Maud wouldn't be needing it any more, but when Mummy put on her that's-enough voice, that was enough.

After the funeral, everyone drove to Uncle Jack and Aunt Janet's house, where they found lots and lots of lovely things to eat: sandwiches full of egg and cheese and lettuce and ham, cakes full of chocolate and cream and jam, biscuits, fruit, orange juice . . .

'Gosh!' said Jeremy James, 'this is a nice party!'

'Now you go and play with Melissa,' said Mummy.

'Oh I don't want to play with *her*,' said Jeremy James, 'I want to stay here by the table and eat all . . .'

'Off you go,' said Mummy.

But before Jeremy James could off-you-go even if he'd wanted to, which he didn't, he found himself face to waistcoat with a very, very, very old man whose tree-root hand came to rest upon his head, and whose watery blue eyes came to rest, one on his face and one round about his right shoulder. 'So this is your little boy, eh?' said a high creaky-door voice.

'That's right, Uncle Albert. This is Jeremy James. Jeremy James, this is your Great-Uncle Albert.'

'Hello,' said Jeremy James. 'You must be very old.'

'How old do you think I am?' said Great-Uncle Albert.

'Oh you must be at least a hundred,' said Jeremy James.

'Hmmph,' said Great-Uncle Albert, 'well I'm not that old, thank you very much.'

'How old *are* you then?' said Jeremy James.

'Jeremy James!' said Mummy.

'That's all right, my dear,' said Great-Uncle Albert, 'if the boy wants to know how old I am, I'll tell him how old I am, if I can remember how old I am. Let's see now, I was born in . . .' Great-Uncle Albert mumbled and muttered a sort of magic spell like 'O three seventy take away worple and add what you first thought of' and moved his tree-root down to Jeremy James's shoulder. 'Seventy-one!' he said, 'that's how old I am. Seventy-one!'

'Gosh!' said Jeremy James, 'you *are* old. You must be almost as old as Great-Aunt Maud.'

'Ah!' said Great-Uncle Albert, 'I couldn't be as old as her, because she was my mother.'

'You . . . you haven't got a mother, have you?' said Jeremy James, eyes as wide as jam tarts.

'Not now,' said Great-Uncle Albert.

'You look much too old to have a mother,' said Jeremy James, 'and that's a fact. Anyway, now that your mother's dead, she won't be needing her box any more, will she?'

'What box?' said Great-Uncle Albert, proving yet again that grown-ups never even notice the most important things in life.

'The box they threw away this afternoon,' said Jeremy James. 'With her in it.'

'Jeremy James,' said Mummy, 'I think you should go and play with Melissa now, dear. That's enough chatter for today.'

'But . . .'

'Off you go, dear.'

'I wanted . . .'

'And here's a nice piece of cream cake for you. Now go and play with Melissa.'

And Jeremy James found his mouth full to overflowing with cake, and he just couldn't say another word.

'What was that about a box?' he heard Great-Uncle Albert say.

'No idea,' said Mummy, 'you know how children talk.'

Jeremy James would have explained it to Great-Uncle Albert, but with a mouth full of cake, a chocolate biscuit in one hand and Mummy's hand in his other hand, he simply didn't have the chance to. Grown-ups are like that sometimes — when there's a really interesting subject to talk about, they tell you to keep quiet. But Mummy did give him a lot more cream cakes and chocolate biscuits, and he didn't have to play with Melissa after all because Melissa was sick and had to go up to her room, and when they were leaving, Uncle Jack pressed tenpence into his hand and said, 'Here you are, Jeremy James, buy yourself some sweets with that.' And when Great-Uncle Albert also gave him tenpence (proving once more that uncles are full of good ideas), he knew for certain that this was the best party he'd ever been to.

85

'Mummy,' he said as Daddy angrily hooted the crowds of people walking in the road outside the football stadium, 'I do like funerals. I hope someone else dies soon, so we can go to another one. Maybe Great-Uncle Albert'll die soon — he looks old enough.'

'That's not a very nice thing to say, dear,' said Mummy. 'You mustn't wish people would die.'

'What happened?' said Daddy through the window to a red-faced man with a moustache who was just over-taking the car.

'Lost,' said the red-faced man. 'Four-nil.'

'Hmmph,' said Daddy. 'Four-nil. They should shoot the lot of 'em!'

'That's not a very nice thing to say,' said Jeremy James — but Daddy didn't seem to hear, and Mummy was suddenly coughing into her handkerchief.

A Birth in the Family

Mummy wasn't well. Mummy hadn't been well for ages. Jeremy James thought she must have eaten an *enormous* number of sweets to be sick for such a long time, but Mummy only smiled and said it wasn't sweets at all. But Mummy's tummy was getting so big that Jeremy James didn't see what else it could possibly be, and he told Daddy what he thought, and Daddy only smiled and said the same as Mummy. And then Daddy looked at Mummy, and Mummy looked at Daddy, and they both smiled, and nodded, and then Mummy said to Jeremy James:

'Jeremy James, how would you like a little brother or sister?'

And Jeremy James thought for a minute or two, and said, 'Well, I'd rather have some strawberries and ice-cream.'

'Well if you're a very good boy,' said Mummy, 'we might let you have a brother *and* some strawberries and ice-cream.'

This sounded rather interesting, and Jeremy James thought for another minute or two. 'Um,' he said — 'um' being his very own word used specially to prepare the way for a request which was unlikely to be granted — 'um . . . can I have the strawberries and ice-cream first, then?'

'You can have strawberries and ice-cream for your tea today,' said Mummy, 'but you won't be getting your brother for quite a while yet.'

'Your sister,' said Daddy.

'Brother,' said Mummy.

And there really *were* strawberries and ice-cream for tea, and Mummy felt much better, and Daddy kept jumping up and down to get things for Mummy, and Jeremy James kept jumping up and down to get things for Jeremy James, and it was a very jolly tea.

'Jeremy James,' said Daddy, 'which would you prefer, a brother or a sister?'

'A brother,' said Jeremy James. 'Because brothers are boys, and I'm a boy, and boys are best 'cos girls are silly.'

'Bad luck,' said Daddy, 'because it's a little girl called Jennifer, and that's a fact.'

'It's a little boy called Christopher,' said Mummy.

'Maybe the man in the baby shop'll tell you,' said Jeremy James, though he wasn't too hopeful about that, as men in shops don't usually tell you very much, except to mind where you're going, or to take your hands off the clothes/toys/chocolate biscuits.

Mummy suddenly said 'Ow!' and put her hand on her tummy.

'What is it, dear?' said Daddy, and did a cow-jumping-over-the-moon leap round the table.

'He kicked me!' said Mummy.

'She kicked you?' said Daddy.

'He did,' said Mummy.

'Did she?' said Daddy.

'Yes,' said Mummy.

And Jeremy James said nothing, because he was wondering just how Mummy could have been kicked

when there was nobody in sight who might have kicked
her. He and Daddy had certainly been over on the other
side of the table, a quick look proved that there was nobody else *under* the table, and Jeremy James knew for a
fact that there was nobody else in the room. Mummy
really *was* ill.

'Come here, Jeremy James,' said Mummy. 'Come
quickly.'

Jeremy James came sort of slowly-quickly to Mummy,
making quite sure on his way that there definitely wasn't

anybody within kicking distance. Mummy took hold of his hand and placed it on her tummy.

'Feel that,' she said.

And then a very strange thing happened. From under Mummy's dress something seemed to jump up against Jeremy James's hand, and it was just like a little kick.

'Did you feel it?' said Mummy.

And Jeremy James looked at her, wide-eyed . . . and felt another leapy-kicky-hiccuppy sort of jerk against his hand. 'That's your little brother,' said Mummy. 'He's inside there, having a good kick.'

'But Mummy,' said Jeremy James, 'what's he doing under your dress?'

'He's not under my dress,' said Mummy. 'He's . . . he's . . . well, you explain it to him, dear.'

'No, you explain it,' said Daddy.

'You explain it,' said Mummy. 'You're better at these things than I am.'

'What things?' said Daddy.

'These things,' said Mummy. 'Things that need to be explained.'

Then Daddy explained to Jeremy James — while Mummy explained to Daddy — how babies grew inside their Mummy's tummy until they were big enough to come out . . . like an egg in a chicken . . . no, not quite like Number Two . . . well sort of . . . no, like an egg in a chicken but we'll get you a book when you're a bit older and that'll explain it much better . . .

'Well I don't remember being inside Mummy's tummy,' said Jeremy James.

'You were rather young at the time,' said Daddy.

'I'm too big to go inside Mummy's tummy,' said Jeremy James.

'You are now,' said Daddy, 'but you were small enough then.'

'Well, how do they get out?' said Jeremy James.

'We should never have started this,' said Daddy.

'Go on, tell him,' said Mummy. 'I'll clear the table.'

'No, you tell him, and I'll clear the table,' said Daddy.

'Well when they're ready,' said Mummy, 'they come out through a hole, that's all. And the doctor comes and helps them out.'

'So how do they get in?' said Jeremy James.

'They just grow in there,' said Mummy. 'And when they're big enough they come out. And you'll see, when Christopher comes out, Mummy's tummy will go quite flat again.'

'*Quite* flat?' said Daddy.

'Fairly flat,' said Mummy.

'Well I don't remember being inside,' said Jeremy James, 'and I don't remember coming out either.'

'Well you *were* inside,' said Daddy, 'and you did come out, and that's enough!'

It was usually Mummy who said 'That's enough', but Daddy's voice was just like Mummy's this time, and Jeremy James decided that Daddy's 'That's enough' meant the same as Mummy's, though he would really have liked to find out a bit more about this funny grown-up way of doing things.

And so Jeremy James waited, and every tea-time he watched Mummy's tummy to see if a little boy would pop out of a hole and Mummy's tummy would go flat again, and Mummy kept saying 'Soon!' and Daddy kept saying 'Hmmph!' — and it was all very puzzling, and Jeremy James still thought it would be much simpler if they went and bought their baby at the baby shop. There at least they'd be able to *see* whether it was a

Christopher or a Jennifer, instead of feeling Mummy's tummy and trying to guess whether it was a boy-kick or a girl-kick. Grown-ups always do make simple things complicated.

Jeremy James never did see any babies come out of Mummy's tummy. He just woke up one bright sun-beamy morning and heard all sorts of funny noises coming from Mummy and Daddy's bedroom. And when he peeped in, he saw his old crib standing in the corner (Mummy and Daddy had said he was such a big boy now, he could sleep in a bed like they did), and Daddy was standing next to the crib in the corner, rocking it backwards and forwards, and there was a loud squeaky-squealy-squawky-squally noise coming from the crib, and Daddy was saying, 'Ssshhh now, ssshhh now, do as Daddy tells you!' in the sort of voice he sometimes used when he was mending things like the bathroom lock, and the squeaky-squawky-squealy-squally noise just got louder and louder, until Daddy stopped rocking the crib and said, 'All right, make as much noise as you bloom-ing well like,' and then the noise stopped and the whole room was quiet, except for a soft Little-Bo-Peep sound from Mummy's bed, which meant that Mummy must be fast asleep.

Then Daddy caught sight of Jeremy James, and waved him in.

'Hey,' said Daddy, ever so quietly, 'come and look at Jennifer! But don't wake her!'

And Jeremy James tiptoed over to the corner, held Daddy's hand, and looked into the crib.

'But . . . but which of them,' said Jeremy James, 'is Jennifer?'

'That one,' said Daddy, 'and that one's Christopher. Or is that one Christopher and that one Jennifer? No,

Jennifer's the one with the pink, and Christopher's the one with the blue.'

'Why have we got *two* babies?' said Jeremy James.

'Ah . . . um . . . well, it's all a matter of semantics, or something like that,' said Daddy.

'Oh,' said Jeremy James. 'Well did they both come out of Mummy's tummy?'

'Yes,' said Daddy.

'Were they both in there together?' said Jeremy James.

'Yes,' said Daddy.

'And are we keeping them both?' said Jeremy James.

'Yes,' said Daddy.

Jeremy James looked down at his brother and sister, and up at his Daddy, and across at his Mummy, and he thought for a very long time.

'Daddy,' he said at last, 'if Mummy had room in her tummy for *two* babies, and I was once a baby in Mummy's tummy, where's the *other* baby that I was in Mummy's tummy with?'

'You do like asking questions, don't you?' said Daddy, and looked across at Mummy, but she was still sleeping. 'Well there wasn't another one,' said Daddy. 'You were all alone. Most babies are all alone, but Christopher and Jennifer are . . . well . . . they're twins . . . they're what we call something special.'

'What does "special" mean, Daddy?' said Jeremy James.

'Well, if something is special,' said Daddy, 'it means there's nothing else like it. For instance, you're the only Jeremy James we've got, so you're special.'

'Are you special, too?' said Jeremy James.

'Yes,' said Daddy. 'And so is Mummy. And so are Christopher and Jennifer.'

'Oh, they can't be special,' said Jeremy James, 'because there's two of them.'

'Well,' said Daddy, 'do you know any other babies quite like Christopher and Jennifer?'

'No-o,' said Jeremy James.

'Then that makes them special, too, doesn't it?' said Daddy.

And the more Jeremy James looked at his new brother and sister, the more special they really seemed to be. You certainly wouldn't be able to buy anything like them at the baby shop, and that was a fact.